SCOOBY-DOO!

and the

VAMPIRE'S REVENGE

Written by
James Gelsey

D0829713

For Ryan

First published in this format in 2014 by Curious Fox,
an imprint of Capstone Global Library Limited,
7 Pilgrim Street, London, EC4V 6LB
– Registered company number: 6695582

www.curious-fox.com

The moral rights of the proprietor have been asserted.

Copyright © 2014 Hanna-Barbera.
SCOOBY-DOO and all related characters and elements are
trademarks of and © Hanna-Barbera.
WB SHIELD: ™ & © Warner Bros. Entertainment Inc.
(s14)

CAPG33551

All rights reserved. No part of this publication may be reproduced
in any form or by any means (including photocopying or storing it in
any medium by electronic means and whether or not transiently or incidentally to some other
use of this publication) without the written permission of the copyright owner.

Originated by Capstone Global Library Ltd
Printed and bound in Spain by Grafos S.A.

ISBN 978 1 782 02153 7
18 17 16 15 14
10 9 8 7 6 5 4 3 2 1

A CIP catalogue record for this book is available
from the British Library.

Chapter 1

"**R**ick or reat!" Scooby barked from the back of the Mystery Machine. He held a brown shopping bag over the front seat.

"No treats here, Scooby," Fred said. "Sorry."

"Awwwww," Scooby sighed.

"Like, don't worry, pal," Shaggy said. "We'll have plenty of time to go trick-or-treating later tonight."

"And plenty of time to fill that great big bag," Velma added.

Shaggy reached under the seat. "If you think that's a big bag," he said, "look at this." He showed them a long green bag with an orange pumpkin on it. "Now that's what I call a trick-or-treat bag."

"It looks more like a duffel bag to me," Daphne said.

"Call it whatever you want," Shaggy said. "Just don't call it empty."

Fred steered the Mystery Machine into a car park. "Here we are," he said. "The Brickstone Towers Hotel."

"And we're right on time," Velma added.

"Right on time for what?" Shaggy asked.

"Rick-or-reating?" Scooby asked, wagging his tail.

"Working," Daphne said. "We promised we'd help out at the annual charity auction, remember?"

"Right." Shaggy nodded. "And then we'll go trick-or-treating, Scooby."

"Rokay!" Scooby barked as he jumped out of the van and followed the others across the car park. The gang looked at the big new hotel towering over them. It was the tallest building in town.

"Jinkies," Velma said. "That hotel is even

bigger up close than I imagined."

"And a little spookier, too," Shaggy added.

The gang walked to the hotel entrance. They stopped in front of the revolving doors.
"Now remember, this is a fancy hotel," Daphne said. "Don't cause any trouble."

"Don't worry, Daphne," Shaggy said. "What kind of trouble could we cause here?"

"I don't know," she answered. "And I don't want to find out." She walked through the revolving door, followed by Fred and Velma. Shaggy and Scooby watched them spin around through the door and into the hotel.

"Ready to go for a spin, Scooby?" Shaggy asked. Scooby nodded as he and Shaggy walked through the revolving door. They pushed the door and started moving. Scooby tripped and fell forwards, pushing the door faster. Shaggy managed to jump out into the hotel, but Scooby was trapped. The door spun around faster and faster.

"Relp! Raggy!" Scooby barked.

A young man dressed like a cowboy came running over to the door. He watched Scooby spin around a couple of times. Then, at just the right moment, he reached his arm in and pulled Scooby-Doo to safety.

"Thanks, man," Shaggy said to the cowboy. He patted Scooby-Doo on the head. "Are you all right, Scoob?"

Daphne gave Scooby a stern look. "No trouble?" she asked.

Scooby lowered his head. "Rorry," he said.

"That's okay, Scooby-Doo," Daphne said. Daphne reached over and scratched his head. "It's hard enough using a revolving door with two feet, much less four. Now, let's find the auction so we can keep our promise."

"And keep you two out of trouble," Velma added.

Chapter 2

The gang started walking down the hallway as the cowboy who rescued Scooby ran up to them.

"Excuse me," he said, smiling. He was wearing a shiny brass name tag with the name Benny written on it. "Can I help you find anything?"

"We're looking for the charity auction," Fred said. Then Fred smiled at Benny. "Hey, you're the one who rescued Scooby."

Scooby walked up to Benny and gave him a big lick across the face. "Ranks!" he barked.

"You're welcome," Benny said as he wiped off his face. "Just doing my job. Benny Noonan, at your service. I'm a customer service attendant."

"A what?" Shaggy asked.

"A porter," Velma said.

Benny nodded. "That's right," he said.

"So why are you dressed like a cowboy?" Daphne asked.

"Mr Brickstone's orders," Benny explained. "He expects all the employees to wear a costume at Halloween."

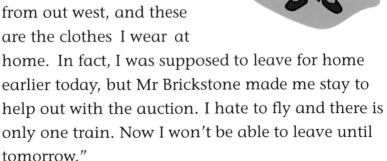

"Those cowboy clothes don't look like a costume to me," Velma said. "They look like real cowboy wear."

"That's because they are," Benny said. "I'm from out west, and these are the clothes I wear at home. In fact, I was supposed to leave for home earlier today, but Mr Brickstone made me stay to help out with the auction. I hate to fly and there is only one train. Now I won't be able to leave until tomorrow."

"That's too bad," Daphne said. "But we're working on the auction, too."

"Then we should go," Benny said. "Mr Brickstone wants to start on time." He led the gang down a wide carpeted hallway. They passed a grand foyer with a crystal chandelier hanging above. Doors to two different ballrooms lined the walls at opposite ends of the room.

"The auction is being held in the Brickstone Ballroom, on the right," Benny explained. "There's a private Halloween party in the Crystal Ballroom, across the foyer." He led the gang through a set of doors into the auction.

The ballroom was enormous. Four giant chandeliers lit the room from above. Rows and rows of chairs were set up facing a stage. On the stage, the gang could see a podium and a large table. A giant banner hung over the stage across the width of the ballroom. BRICKSTONE HALLOWEEN

AUCTION was written on it in big black letters.

"NOO-NAN!" someone bellowed from the far end of the ballroom.

"Y-y-y-yes, sir?" Benny said.

"Who's with you?" the voice barked.

"The v-v-v-volunteers, sir," Benny answered.

"Well, don't just stand there, bring them in," the voice ordered.

"Follow me," Benny said. He walked up the centre aisle between the rows of chairs to the stage. The gang followed. They looked around the room.

"BOO!" the same voice yelled.

"Rikes!" Scooby said, jumping into Shaggy's arms.

A tall man stood up from behind the podium.

He wore grey trousers, with a matching grey shirt and black tie. "Happy Halloween!" he said. "I'm Rock Brickstone. Thank you for volunteering."

"You're welcome, sir," Fred said.

"Only employees have to call me sir," Rock said with a smile. "You can call me Mr Brickstone. Follow me." He walked through a curtain next to the stage. It led to a storage area. There were boxes of all shapes and sizes stacked everywhere.

"These are all the things that are going to be auctioned off tonight," Rock said. "Your job is to make sure that the objects are unpacked and ready for auction. Any questions?"

Before anyone could answer, Rock continued, "Good. The auction will be starting very soon, so you'd better get started." Rock turned to leave and then stopped. "And one more thing," he said. "Everyone in the hotel has to be in costume tonight." Rock looked at Scooby-Doo. "It doesn't have to be as fancy as your buddy here in the dog costume. Anything will do. See you later." Rock left the storage room.

Shaggy and Scooby looked at the boxes piled up around the room.

"Man, we'll be here till next Halloween unpacking these boxes," Shaggy said.

"But the auction is *this* Halloween," Fred said. "And the sooner we get started, the sooner you two can go trick-or-treating."

"Ret's ro!" Scooby barked as he and Shaggy sprang into action.

Chapter 3

Everyone started unpacking the boxes. Daphne opened a box and carefully took out some old dishes and platters. Velma tried to lift what was in her box but couldn't do it.

"Fred, can you give me a hand with this?" she asked. Fred came over and helped Velma lift a big brass lamp out of a box.

"The date stamped here says 1878," Velma commented. "This lamp must be very valuable."

"I think all of this stuff is valuable," Fred added.

"Like, even this?" Shaggy said. He held up a large round medallion with a circle of small green stones in the centre. He noticed some writing on one side. "Listen to this, Scoob." Shaggy tried to read the writing. "Serip mav emoc lew."

Scooby giggled at the sound of the words.

Shaggy shook his head. "Those are some crazy words on one ugly paperweight."

"That is no paperweight," a voice said with a heavy foreign accent. Everyone turned and saw a short man standing there. He was wearing a black satin cape over his tuxedo. A bright yellow VIP badge hung on a gold chain around his neck. "That is the Crostini Medallion."

"Who are you?" Daphne asked.

"I am Lugo Belasi," the man said. "I collect jewels, and other rare items of value. I also happen to be an expert in Transylvanian art."

"Do you mean this medallion is from

Transylvania?" Fred asked.

"Judging by your accent, I'd say you are, also," Velma guessed.

"That is correct," Lugo said. "This medallion is very, very old. It is also very, very cursed. Whoever holds the medallion and reads the inscription will be haunted by a vampire."

"Haunted by a vampire?" Shaggy asked. "Zoinks!" He looked at the medallion in his hand and quickly tossed it over to Scooby.

"Rikes!" Scooby caught it and tossed it back to Shaggy. Shaggy tossed it over his shoulder.

Benny ran over and caught the medallion before it hit the floor.

"Hey, you two, be careful with that," Daphne scolded. "That's for the auction."

"Besides," Velma added, "there's no such thing as vampires."

"I would not be so sure about that," Lugo said. "But I must go now. I only came back here for a quick preview of the auction items." Lugo turned and left the storage room.

"That reminds me," Benny said. "I should go and make sure everything is okay in the lobby.

If you need me, just look for the cowboy."

"I don't know about you guys," Shaggy said, "but I'm not going to wait around for any vampires to come and haunt me. You coming, Scoob?"

"Reah, reah," Scooby barked, nodding.

"Shaggy, for the last time, there's no such thing as vampires," Velma said. "Not in Transylvania and not in this hotel."

The gang heard a stack of boxes fall over behind them. They turned and saw someone standing there.

"Jinkies!" Velma exclaimed.

"Vampire!" Shaggy and Scooby yelled.

Chapter 4

The vampire stared at the gang. Then he narrowed his eyes and hissed right at Shaggy and Scooby.

"That's it!" Shaggy said. "We're outta here!" He and Scooby ran through the curtain and into the main ballroom. It was full of people in costumes waiting for the auction to begin. Shaggy and Scooby found two empty chairs. Two people dressed as witches sat in front of them. Shaggy and Scooby grabbed the witch hats and pulled them low over their faces.

"He won't recognize us in these costumes," Shaggy said. "There's no way he can find us."

Just then the vampire ran onto the stage and roared at the crowd. Everyone screamed and jumped out of their seats.

"Rikes!" Scooby exclaimed. "Re round us!"

"Let's go, Scoob!" Shaggy said. They stood up and ran out of the room as quickly as they could.

Fred ran through the curtain. "Stop that vampire!" he shouted. "He stole the Crostini Medallion!"

Upon hearing this, the vampire ran off the stage, down the centre aisle, and out of the doors.

Just outside the ballroom, Shaggy and Scooby saw a large trolley of food draped with a white tablecloth.

"I've got an idea, Scooby," Shaggy said. "Follow me." Shaggy got down and crawled under the trolley. Scooby followed but managed to grab a plate of food on the way.

"Nice going, Scooby," Shaggy whispered.

"This running from vampires sure makes me hungry."

"Me roo," Scooby agreed.

The trolley started slowly moving.

"Sit back and enjoy the ride, Scooby," Shaggy said. "No vampire will find us under here."

The vampire burst out of the Brickstone Ballroom as the trolley was being rolled into the Crystal Ballroom. The vampire ran into the Crystal Ballroom, too, just as Fred, Daphne, and Velma came into the hallway.

"We'd better hurry before he leaves the other ballroom," Fred said. The three of them marched into the Crystal Ballroom.

"Oh, no!" Daphne exclaimed. "It's a costume party."

"And everyone's dressed like a vampire!" Velma added.

Hundreds of people dressed as vampires walked and danced around the ballroom. There were tall vampires and short vampires, skinny vampires and fat vampires. One of the vampires walked up to Fred.

"Welcome," he said, "to the Dracula Spectacular! And what kind of vampires are you supposed to be?"

"We're not supposed to be any kind of vampires," Velma said.

"We're looking for someone," Fred added. "But we'll never find him now."

"Well, it's Halloween, so make yourselves at home," the man said as he walked away. "Help yourself to some Dracula snackulas."

Fred, Daphne, and Velma noticed a food trolley off to one side of the room. Suddenly they saw a paw come up from under the trolley and grab some food. They all looked at one another and smiled.

"Seems like Shaggy and Scooby have already made themselves at home," Daphne said. She walked over and lifted the tablecloth. Shaggy and Scooby were sitting under the trolley, munching away.

"Oh, hi, Daph," Shaggy said, chewing on a sandwich. "Don't blow our cover. We don't want any vampires to find us."

"Then you sure picked the wrong party to crash," Velma said as she walked over. "Take a look around."

Shaggy and Scooby leaned out from under the cart and looked around the room.

"Like, what is this place, the vampire state building?" Shaggy asked. He pulled the tablecloth back down.

Daphne lifted the cloth back up. "It's a party for people dressed up as vampires," she said.

"I have a hunch our mystery vampire knew exactly where to go to hide," Velma said. "I think we should look for clues somewhere else instead."

"Great idea, Velma," Fred said, nodding. "Let's go. And that includes you, Shaggy and Scooby."

Chapter 5

The gang walked back out into the foyer between the two ballrooms.

"There aren't a lot of places where the vampire could have gone," Velma said.

"Right," Fred agreed. "Daphne and I will look around the storage area."

"I want to see if there are any other ways out of that ballroom," Velma said.

"Scooby and I will check out something else," Shaggy said.

"What?" Fred asked.

"Like, out of this hotel!" Shaggy replied. He and Scooby laughed as Benny came out of the Brickstone Ballroom.

"Hi, Benny," Daphne said. "How are things in there?"

"Everyone's calmed down," Benny said. "They're going to start the auction pretty soon."

"Then we don't have much time," Fred said.

"Once the auction starts, Mr Brickstone is going to want us to get back to work. So let's get started."

"Started with what?" Benny asked.

"Looking for clues to this vampire mystery," Velma replied. "And we could use your help."

"Really? I'd love to," Benny said. "But I have to stick around here and wait for Mr Brickstone to come back."

"Then can you tell me where I can find the back door to the Crystal Ballroom?" Velma asked.

27

"I want to see how the vampire could have got out."

"Sure," Benny answered. "Just go down that hall, turn left, and—" Benny stopped talking as he noticed someone walking down the hall. "Gotta go!" He quickly turned and went back into the ballroom.

"Like, what got into him?" Shaggy asked. "He looks like he's seen a ghost."

"Well, I'm sure I can find my way," Velma said. "I'll meet up with you later." She turned and walked off.

"What are you kids doing out here?" a man asked from behind them. Fred, Daphne, Shaggy, and Scooby all jumped and then turned around.

"Mr Brickstone!" Daphne said.

"Well?" he said impatiently.

"We were just making sure everything was ready for the auction to start," Fred said.

"Well, it is," Mr Brickstone said. "I've taken care of this mysterious vampire. It was one of our hotel residents playing a practical joke. Now please return to the storage room. I don't want to risk losing any more of those antiques."

"We're on our way," Daphne said.

Mr Brickstone turned and walked away.

"Well, it sounds to me like this mystery's solved," Shaggy said. "Time to go."

"Rick-or-reating?" Scooby asked, his tail wagging happily.

"Not so fast, you two," Fred said. "I think there's something more going on here. You should go find Velma and see if she needs help. Daphne and I will handle everything in here for the auction."

"All right," Shaggy said, "but, like, don't blame us if we don't make it back because the vampire got us. Come on, Scoob."
The two of them moped down the hallway.

Fred and Daphne went back to the storage room. They looked around the jumble of boxes on the floor where the vampire had first appeared. Daphne pushed one aside and something white caught her eye. She knelt down to get a closer look.

"Fred," Daphne called. "Take a look at this." She pointed to three white footprints on the floor.

"It looks like someone walked in some kind of white powder," Fred said.

"And walked right out of the wall," Daphne said. "Look how close this footprint is to the wall."

"We need brass lamp, item number ten!" someone called from outside the storage room. "Coming up next for the auction."

"I'll be right back," Fred said. He got up and went to look for the brass lamp.

Daphne knelt down by the wall next to the footprint for a closer look. She put her hand against the wall for support and heard a soft *click*. The wall gave way and opened like a door. Daphne lost her balance and fell all the way into the doorway. The door snapped shut behind her. Daphne was trapped behind the wall.

Chapter 6

Shaggy and Scooby continued along the hotel hallway.

"We're never going to find Velma like this," Shaggy said. "Looks like it's time for some Scooby sniffing."

"Right," Scooby said. He put his nose to the ground and started sniffing around. Then he picked up a scent. "Ris way," he barked. Scooby followed the scent and Shaggy followed Scooby.

Scooby led Shaggy down the hallway, then left, then right, then up some stairs and down some others. They went through a series of doors until Shaggy had no idea where they were anymore. The scent got stronger, and Scooby started walking faster. Shaggy had to jog just to keep up.

Scooby finally stopped in front of a lift.

"Like, are we there yet?" Shaggy asked.

Before Scooby could answer, the lift doors opened. Scooby put his head in the lift and took a big sniff.

"Rin rere," he barked. Shaggy and Scooby walked into the lift. The doors closed and the lift started moving.

"I hope you know where you're going, Scooby-Doo," Shaggy said. The lift stopped and the doors opened.

Scooby looked up. "Rikes!" he barked.

It was the vampire! He raised his arms in his big black cape and hissed at Shaggy and Scooby.

"Let's get out of here!" Shaggy yelled. He and Scooby ran between the vampire's legs and down the hall. The vampire started to chase them but stopped when he heard a noise. A hotel guest unlocked his door and stuck his head out into the hallway. He was also dressed as a vampire, but he smiled at Shaggy and Scooby. The other vampire quickly jumped into the lift.

When they heard the lift doors close, Shaggy and Scooby stopped to catch their breath.

"Boy, that was close," Shaggy said. "If I see one more vampire, I don't know what I'll do."

They heard a door open behind them. A short, stocky man dressed as a vampire came out.

"On second thoughts, I know exactly what I'll do," Shaggy said. He and Scooby looked at each other. "Run!" they yelled.

Shaggy and Scooby ran back down the hall towards the lift. As they arrived, the doors opened. Another person dressed as a vampire stepped out.

"Here we go again," Shaggy said. He and

Scooby dived between the person's legs and into the lift. The doors closed and the lift started moving.

"As soon as these doors open, Scooby," Shaggy said, "we're gone!"

The lift stopped but the doors didn't open. Instead, a set of doors behind them opened. Shaggy and Scooby rubbed their eyes.

"Like, forget what I just said," Shaggy remarked. "This place doesn't seem so terrible after all."

"Rou raid it!" Scooby said. His big pink tongue swept across his mouth and nose.

Shaggy and Scooby stepped out of the lift and found themselves in one of the hotel's kitchens!

"I think this is as good a place as any to look for clues, right, Scoob?" Shaggy said. "Right, Raggy," Scooby barked.

"I'll look in the refrigerator," Shaggy said. "You look in the cupboards over there." Shaggy walked over to the fridge and opened the doors. "Hmmm. These leftovers look very suspicious," he said. "I'd better have a look at them." Shaggy started gathering things together to make a sandwich.

Meanwhile, Scooby walked over to the cupboards. He opened one and found a lot of tinned fruits and vegetables. Scooby looked inside the cupboard door and noticed an apron and a chef's hat hanging on a hook. He reached for the apron and hat and put them on. As Scooby walked over to Shaggy, the hook popped up and the back of the cupboard suddenly opened.

Shaggy was putting the finishing touches on his quadruple-decker sandwich. "Hey, Scoob, did you find anything suspicious and delicious?" Shaggy asked.

"Just me!" someone said from behind them.

Shaggy and Scooby spun around.

"Daphne!" Shaggy exclaimed. "Where did you come from?"

"From inside that cupboard," she replied. "And not a moment too soon."

Chapter 7

"I was trapped in a secret passage behind the storage room," Daphne explained. "Just before Scooby opened the cupboard, I heard someone else walking behind me."

Shaggy, Daphne, and Scooby could hear the sound of footsteps coming out of the secret passage.

"Sounds like he's getting closer," Daphne said. "What are we going to do?"

"I've got one word of advice for times like these," Shaggy said. "Hide!" He and Scooby dived behind the counter. Daphne picked up a frying pan and stood just outside the cupboard. The

footsteps grew louder and then stopped just inside the doorway. A figure stepped out of the shadows.

"Fred!" Daphne exclaimed. "What are you doing here?" She put down the frying pan.

"After you disappeared, I finally got the secret door to open," he explained. "Now that I know where it leads, it makes perfect sense."

Velma stepped out of the lift just as Fred was finishing. "What makes perfect sense?" she asked.

Fred and Daphne turned around and saw Velma standing there. Shaggy and Scooby peeked over the worktop.

"Fred? Velma? Like, it's a regular re-union," Shaggy said. "This calls for a celebration. Sandwiches for everyone!" He and Scooby got back to work making sandwiches.

"What did you find?" Velma asked.

"Daphne found this secret passage that leads from here to the storage room," Fred explained.

"That would explain how the vampire got into the room without us knowing," Daphne said. "But we also found some white footprints."

"The vampire probably got flour on his shoes before he entered the passage," Fred pointed out.

"Look what else I found in the secret passage," Daphne said. She held out half of a torn yellow VIP pass. "Whoever this vampire is," she added, "he clearly knows his way around the hotel."

"And he has VIP access to everywhere," Velma said. "I looked in the service hallway behind that vampire party. I found a room key that opened a hotel room on the VIP floor."

"Like, what does VIP stand for?" Shaggy asked. "Vampires Invade Parties?"

"Very Important People," Velma explained. "They have a separate floor of the hotel reserved for them. That's where this lift goes. And that's where I found a couple of things. First I found the Crostini Medallion's carrying case. Then I found a piece of paper with airline flights to and from Transylvania listed. And scribbled on the back of the paper were the names and phone numbers of hotels there."

"Since when do vampires need aeroplanes to fly?" Shaggy asked. "Like, aren't they supposed to be able to turn into bats and fly on their own?"

"You're right, Shaggy," Velma said. "Something tells me it's time to clip this vampire's wings."

Fred agreed. "And time to set a trap."

"I'm going to start in the lobby," Velma said as she walked to the lift. "I'll meet the rest of you back in the storage room."

Chapter 8

"**W**e have to head back to the storage room now," Fred said. "Sorry, Scooby-Doo, but there won't be time for you to finish your sandwich."

Scooby looked at his sandwich. He had only taken one bite.

"Like, no problem, Fredaroony," Shaggy said. "Right, Scoob?"

"Right!" Scooby barked. Scooby opened his mouth extra wide. He flattened his sandwich between his front paws until it fit into his mouth.

Then he gulped it down. "Ahhhhh," he sighed as he rubbed his belly. "Ret's ro!"

"Daphne, since you've been through the passage once, you lead the way," Fred said. "I'll stay in the back to make sure no one follows us."

Daphne walked up to the doorway. "Okay, boys, there's nothing to be afraid of in here." Daphne entered the secret passage.

"Who's afraid? I'm not afraid," Shaggy said. "You first, Scooby." He pushed Scooby ahead of him into the passage.

After they came out into the storage room, Fred made sure the secret door closed.

"When the vampire shows up again, we'll be ready," Fred said.

"Like, how do you know he'll show up again?" Shaggy asked. "Not that I would mind if he didn't."

"Oh, he'll show up all right," Velma said, walking into the room. "That's what I did in the lobby. I told some people another valuable medallion was just added to the auction."

"Not another medallion," Shaggy moaned. "Be sure to keep it away from Scooby and me."

"Shaggy, there is no other medallion. Velma just made it up," Daphne said. "Only the vampire doesn't know that. He'll think there's another valuable object here and try to grab it."

"Which is when we'll grab him," Fred continued. "That's where you come in, Shaggy and Scooby."

Shaggy and Scooby looked at each other.

"I don't like the sound of that," Shaggy said.

"I asked Benny to come back here with a couple of costumes for you two," Velma said. "You'll put them on and hide in the audience with the rest of the bidders. When the vampire shows up here, we'll chase him out onto the stage and you two will grab him."

Scooby started shaking his head. "Roh ray," he barked.

"Will you do it for a Scooby Snack?" Daphne asked.

"Rope!" Scooby said. "Roh rampires!"

"How about for two Scooby Snacks?" Daphne said.

"Ruh-ruh."

"How about for two Scooby Snacks and my whole trick-or-treat bag from later on tonight?" Velma said.

Scooby's eyes lit up. "Rick-or-reats? Rou bet!" he barked as his tail wagged happily.

Velma tossed two Scooby Snacks into the air. Scooby jumped up and gobbled them down with one gulp.

Benny walked into the storage room carrying two costumes.

"We didn't have any more costumes," he said. "So I had to settle for these uniforms instead. Since the whole staff is wearing Halloween costumes tonight, I had a big selection to choose from. I hope they fit. By the way, there's a big crowd coming back into the ballroom. People are talking about another medallion that was just added to the auction."

"Great," Fred said. "That means we don't have much time. You two better put on those costumes and get outside quick."

Shaggy and Scooby put on their costumes. Scooby was dressed as a porter, complete with a little red hat. Shaggy wore a dark blue doorman's jacket with gold braids on the sleeve and lots of shiny brass buttons. They walked out into the ballroom and sat in two empty seats.

A moment later, Shaggy and Scooby heard noises coming from the storage room. The vampire ran out of the storage room and onto the auction stage. He was looking for the other medallion.

"Get him!" Fred yelled as he ran out of the

storage room.

"That's our cue, Scooby-Doo," Shaggy said. He and Scooby sprang up and ran- towards the vampire just as he jumped off the stage. Now the vampire was running right at them.

"Rikes!" Scooby yelled.

"About-face!" Shaggy yelled. He and Scooby turned around and started running away from the vampire. They ran down the centre aisle and out of the ballroom. Out in the hallway, they spotted the food cart from earlier that night.

"Under here, Scoob!" Shaggy said as he lifted up the white cloth covering the trolley. Scooby was about to dive under the trolley when he felt the

vampire grab his tail. Scooby managed to grab hold of one end of the trolley. Shaggy grabbed the other end of the trolley and pulled. Scooby was being stretched like a piece of elastic.

"Relp! Raggy!" Scooby barked. The vampire gave a hard yank. Shaggy lost his balance and let go of the trolley. The trolley shot forward towards the vampire, who lost his grip on Scooby's tail. Scooby jumped on top of the trolley as it rolled faster and faster after the vampire.

The vampire ran down the hall and turned to look behind him. He saw the trolley and Scooby-Doo gaining speed. He also saw Scooby-Doo cover his eyes and suddenly jump off. The vampire looked forward and saw the hotel's revolving door in front of him. He ran right into the revolving door and spun round and round.

Chapter 9

When the revolving door stopped spinning, the vampire staggered out and collapsed onto the lobby floor. Everyone came running out into the lobby.

"Now we'll see who the vampire really is," Velma said.

Fred reached over and removed the vampire's mask.

"Mr Brickstone!" Benny gasped from behind Fred. "You're the vampire?"

"Just as we suspected," Velma said. "Of course, he wasn't our first guess."

"Who was?" Benny asked.

"You were," Fred replied.

"Why me?" Benny asked.

"Because you seemed really unhappy about having to work on Halloween," Daphne told him. "And you know all of the back doors and secret ins and outs of the hotel."

"But when we found the airline information for Transylvania, we knew you couldn't have been the vampire," Fred said. "You're afraid of flying, right? That's why you were going to take the train

to visit your family."

"So you went from a porter to me?" Rock Brickstone asked.

"Not quite," Velma continued. "We thought Lugo Belasi was guilty. After all, the key I found was to his hotel room on the VIP level. He seemed to know an awful lot about the medallion. But the information we found also had phone numbers of hotels on it."

"So?" Rock said. "What does that prove?"

"It proves that whoever was flying to Transylvania needed a place to stay," Daphne replied. "People who live in Transylvania – like Lugo Belasi – don't need to stay in hotels in Transylvania."

"You planted those things in Lugo's room to make it look like he took the medallion," Fred said. "You even told us that you had found out a hotel resident was responsible."

"You just didn't mention that *you* were that hotel resident," Daphne added.

The hotel security guards came over to the crowd. Lugo Belasi was with them.

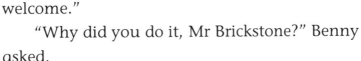

"Remember those words on the medallion?" Lugo asked. "In Transylvanian, the words mean 'vampires welcome.' But *this* vampire has worn out his welcome."

"Why did you do it, Mr Brickstone?" Benny asked.

"I did it so I could turn the Brickstone Towers Hotel into an international chain of luxury hotels," he answered. "That medallion would have given me the money and status I needed to start building hotels around the world."

"But what about the charity auction?" Lugo asked.

"I had to do something to make me look respectable," Rock replied. "Believe me, I didn't enjoy it. All I can say is that I would have got away with everything if it weren't for those kids and their meddling mutt."

Rock Brickstone winced as the hotel security guards put handcuffs on him and took him away.

"Speaking of our meddling mutt, has anyone seen Scooby?" Shaggy asked. Everyone shook their heads.

"Scooby-Doo, where are you?" Shaggy called.

"Rover rere," Scooby answered. Shaggy followed Scooby's voice and found his friend sitting in an enormous bowl of Halloween candy the hotel had put out for its guests.

"Are you okay, Scoob?" Shaggy asked.

"Rick or reat!" Scooby barked.

Shaggy jumped into the bowl with Scooby. "And Happy Halloween to you, Scooby-Doo!"

Solve a Mystery With Scooby-Doo!

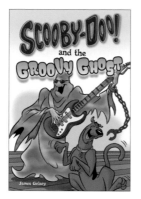

978-1-782-02155-1

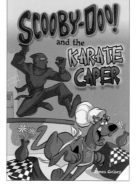

978-1-782-02150-6

978-1-782-02152-0

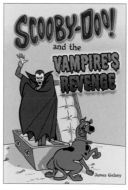

978-1-782-02153-7